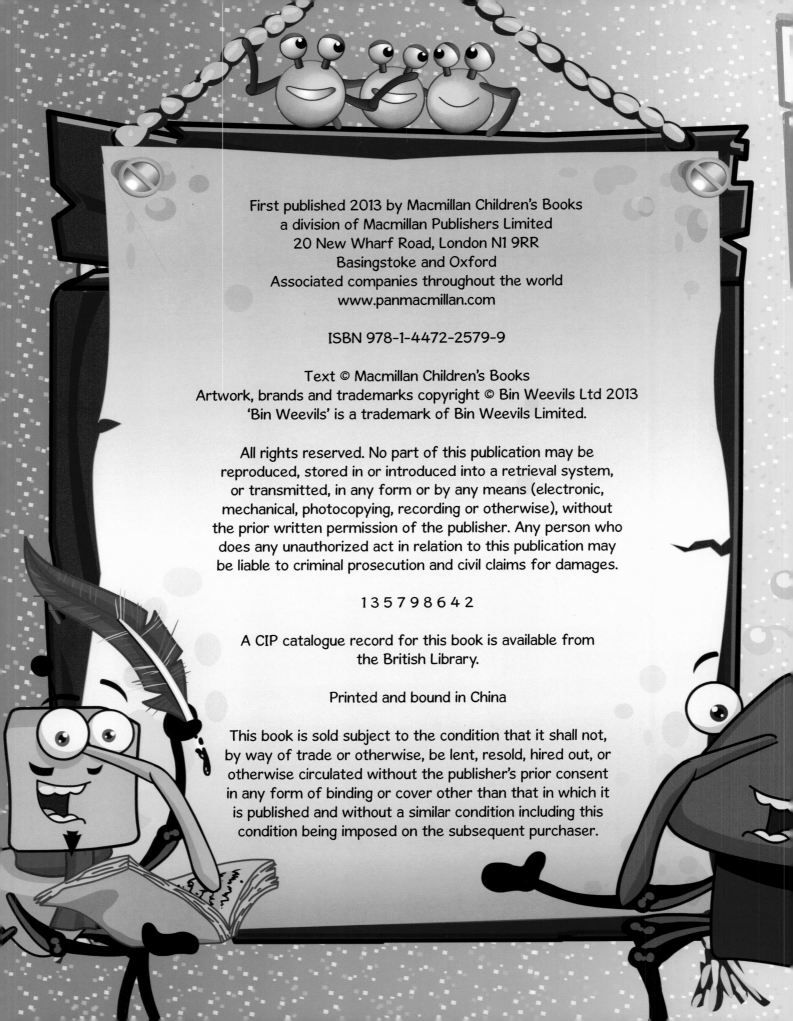

First published 2013 by Macmillan Children's Books
a division of Macmillan Publishers Limited
20 New Wharf Road, London N1 9RR
Basingstoke and Oxford
Associated companies throughout the world
www.panmacmillan.com

ISBN 978-1-4472-2579-9

Text © Macmillan Children's Books
Artwork, brands and trademarks copyright © Bin Weevils Ltd 2013
'Bin Weevils' is a trademark of Bin Weevils Limited.

1 3 5 7 9 8 6 4 2

A CIP catalogue record for this book is available from
the British Library.

Printed and bound in China

CONTENTS

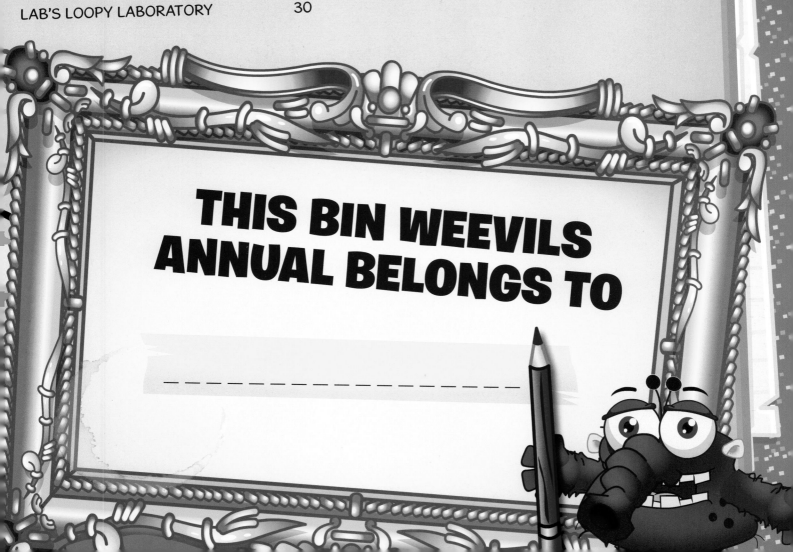

THIS BIN WEEVILS ANNUAL BELONGS TO

DIGG'S DIG

Hi, there! I'm Digg, the Bin's favourite archaeologist. Well, it's not like there are that many of us, but I'm sure I'd make the grade anyway — because I lurrrve dirt and all the cool ancient things you can find buried in it!

I've been working on Mulch Island for months, excavating some of those fascinating old ruins. It's taking a good ol' while, what with the WEB always getting in the way . . . but I've made some seriously Bin-tacular finds!

Unfortunately, I made the mistake of asking Tink and Clott to bring back one of my finds to the mainland for me. Can you believe it? Hand them ONE priceless artefact to take care of, and those Bin-brains go and lose pieces of it all over the place! Who knows where they all are now!

Help us! Can you find the missing pieces of this mosaic?

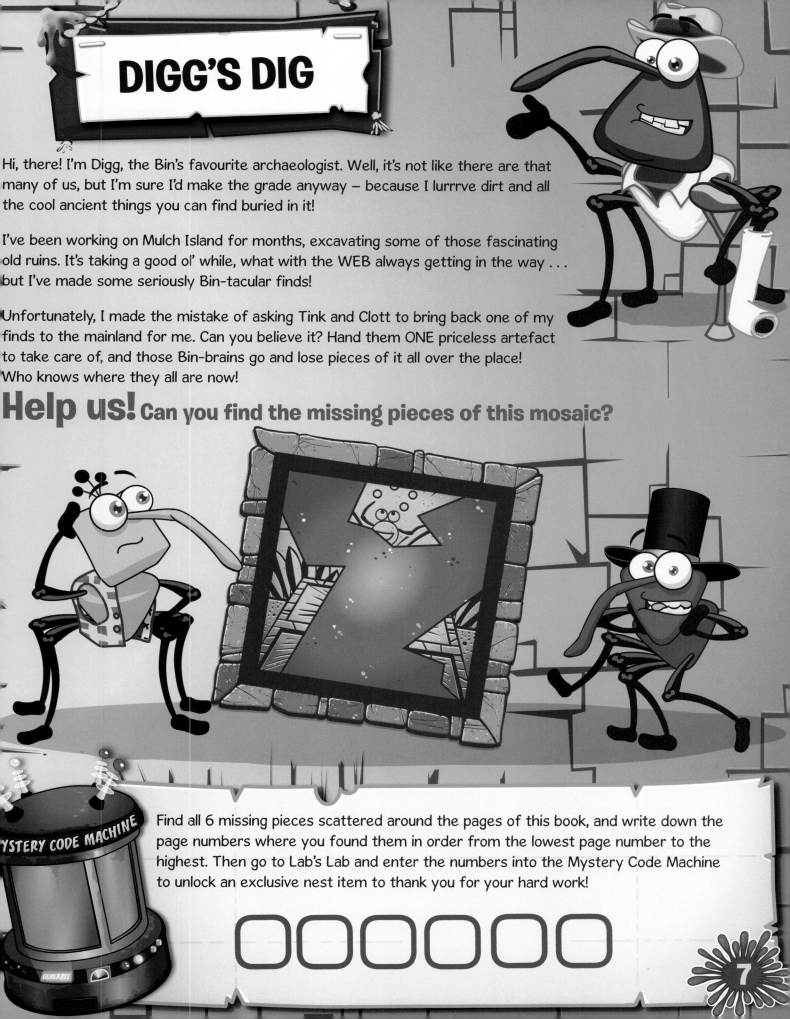

Find all 6 missing pieces scattered around the pages of this book, and write down the page numbers where you found them in order from the lowest page number to the highest. Then go to Lab's Lab and enter the numbers into the Mystery Code Machine to unlock an exclusive nest item to thank you for your hard work!

MYSTERY CODE MACHINE

GENERATE

7

NEW YEAR, NEW LOOK!

NEST INSPECTOR'S TOP TIPS TO FRESHEN UP YOUR NEST

Giving your nest a new look doesn't have to mean spending like a Mulch millionaire!
Take a look through your My Stuff Box and see what magic you can do with the nest
items you already have!

CLEAROUT TIME!

TOP TIP:
Take a trip to the Haggle Hut and clear out any items you don't use. All that bonus Mulch will come in handy if you want some new stuff!

BRIGHTEN THINGS UP!

A dull nest room can easily be brightened up by some carefully placed lights! Add a candle, a lamp or some hanging lights to give your room some glow!

COORDINATE!

TOP TIP:
For an ultra-coordinated room, choose one or two main focus colours, then add nest items in similar tones. For a finishing touch, add some trophies that match!

FLIP YOUR COLOURS!

Sometimes a change of colour is all it takes to make a nest room feel fresh and new! I swapped all the red items in this room for green ones and — hey presto — a whole new look. Check out this weevily amazing transformation!

I'd like to start the year off with these Bin-tastic items!

HIP HAT

NATTY NEST ITEM

PERFECT PLANT

9

BUNTY'S SECRETS

Hi, I'm Bunty! You've probably seen me backstage at the Bin's coolest gigs, or maybe even working a red carpet or two. No matter what's going on in the Binscape, you bet I've got the inside info . . . you could say I'm a gossip guru! Here are some of the hottest secrets I've unearthed recently about my favourite celebs. Juicy!

Mega-wealthy Dosh can't stand dirty Mulch notes, but did you know he also hates creases? He insists on ironing all the tablecloths in the Palace himself because no one can do as good a job on those crisp edges!

Bin diva Song has a big voice and an even bigger list of demands when she plays a gig! One of the things she asks for is a Slime Sandwich sliced into quarters with the crusts cut off and exactly three and a half dollops of mustard.

Speed-demon Ham has seven strange lucky charms that he thinks bring him good fortune on the track. They're a closely guarded secret, but I can reveal that one of them is a straw from the smoothie he drank on the morning of his first big victory!

BLING'S FAVOURITE THINGS

Bling loves everything that shimmers and shines and she's got the Bin's biggest stockpile of glitter! Here's some of her favourite sparkly stuff!

RUBY SUNGLASSES

Bling feels like a superstar when she's rocking these sweet shades.

DIAMOND CROWN

Bling hardly ever goes out without her trademark monogrammed cowboy hat, but for special occasions nothing beats this luminescent lid!

LEVEL 49 TROPHY

A level trophy covered with giant gems? Yes, please! The day she got this trophy was a Bin-tastic day indeed!

JEWELLED BIN PET BOWL

Bling's Bin Pet dines in sparkling style . . . even Lady Wawa doesn't have a bowl as fancy as this one!

BLING MUSHROOM & BLING TREE

You'd better believe her garden's aglow with oodles of these jewel-encrusted plants!

BLOOMIN' BINCARDS

Ooh la la!
Aren't these lovely? The seeds for these super-exclusive rare plants can only be found by stamping special spaces on your BinCard! Have you collected all of these seeds and more?

BinCard #11

MY VOUCHERS   MY PUZZLES

Magician Tree
This tree's got a few tricks up its sleeve . . . Well, it certainly would if trees had sleeves!

Octo-Cactus
More dangerous than the Venus Flytrap . . . watch out for those spiny tentacles! Ouch!

Crab Tree
Despite its name, this tree isn't crabby at all. In fact, it's downright cheerful!

Butterfishy

An unusual oddball that will make your Bin Garden a top attraction! Splish, splash, flutter!

Rocket

Blast your garden into the space race when you find this cosmically cool secret seed!

Mega-Sunflower

This gargantuan bloom has a king-sized personality to match its mass!

Totem Pole Plant

Have you spotted some of your favourite celebs' faces on this VIP plant?

Draw your idea for a crazy new BinCard plant here!

FLEM'S WORD PUZZLES

Flem here, wordsmith extraordinaire! Excuse the mess . . . I'm making over my Manor to keep up with that bigwig, Dosh. Sure, he's got his shiny gold trimmings and his fancy architecture, but my Manor's got character . . . and a Bin-tastic library! Here's a list of things I need for my renovations. Find all the words hidden in the grid below – they read forwards, backwards, up, down and diagonally!

WORDSEARCH

```
H T O L C P O R D S R Y R G X
C N B D T G X W Q S A K U P P
U I N L T Q O B U R J U L T U
K R R A F I B G O G G L E S P
X P P B Q W L E V E L P R D P
R E M M A H O E F W R E C R T
O U S I S F O I S A D D B A Y
Z L L I R D T E C L U O H O X
S B L U B T H G I L R D V B F
F O T N I S G U L P R A E N A
P L D N U L B A V A R N I S H
P O G R I I F R H P A K V S Q
L S B A C A H C N E B K R O W
S W A P W N P R G R J U K S K
P R Z L X L Y I N B X C H X J
```

BLUEPRINT
BOARDS
BRUSHES
BUILDERS
CARPET
DRILL

TAPE
TILES
TOOLBOX
VARNISH
WALLPAPER
WORKBENCH

DROPCLOTH
EARPLUGS
FABRIC
FITTINGS

GOGGLES
HAMMER
HARD HAT
LEVEL
LIGHTBULBS

NAILS
PAINT
POLISH
RULER

Uh-oh! My list of rooms that need redecorating has scrambled up somehow! Can you unjumble the names of the rooms?

CIHKNET _____

LORAURP _____

OMEBRDO _____

RYIRLBA _____

ANIM ALHL _____

TYSDU _____

AEGYLLR _____

GNIDIN OMRO _____

CROSSWORD

Now, you're a whizz! Now can you put that Bin-brain of yours to work and solve this cool crossword? When it's finished, the shaded letters will make up one final word to unscramble!

Shaded letters:

Unscrambled word:

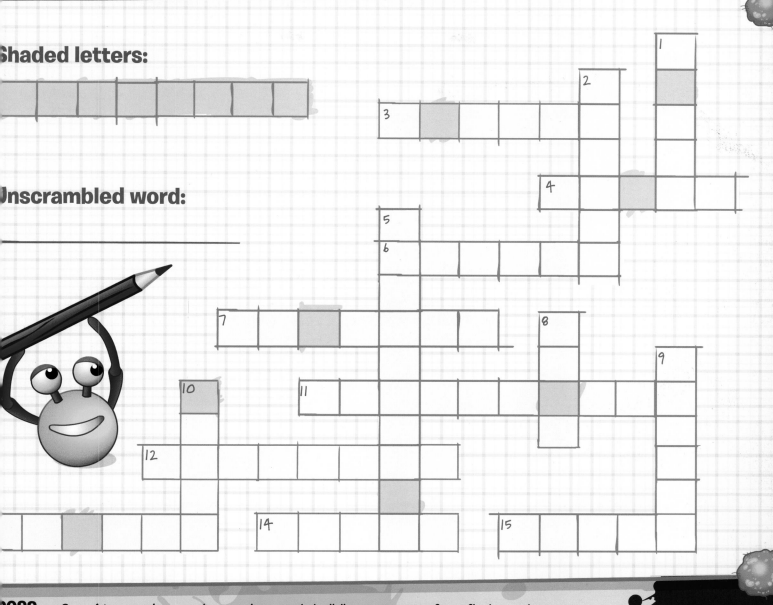

ACROSS

3 At a movie premiere or in a posh building, you can often find a red _ _ _ _ _ _.
4 A kitchen floor is often covered with these.
6 In creaky old houses you can sometimes hear strange _ _ _ _ _ _.
7 This mythical creature doesn't like sunlight!
11 A grand, ornamental light fitting that hangs from the ceiling.
12 This item stands in your garden and spouts water.
13 I think my Manor is haunted, because I've seen a few _ _ _ _ _ _ in the halls!
14 Statues are often carved from this hard grey material.
15 A visitor to your home can also be called a _ _ _ _ _.

DOWN

1 A painting or a photo is usually placed inside a _ _ _ _ _ before being hung up.
2 To get to the next floor, you have to climb up these.
5 You send this to ask your friends to a party.
8 This precious yellow metal is often found in palaces!
9 Someone who paints, sculpts or makes artwork is called an _ _ _ _ _ _.
10 A library is full of lots and lots of these!

15

What Do You Do With A Dragon?

*I*t was during the dark days of the Great Bin War, when I was still a sprightly young Bin Weevil . . . On my way to collect some food and supplies, I'd stopped to rest for the night in a cave. Inside the cave, I'd found something marvellous – a rainbow dragon's egg! It wasn't easy to keep that egg out of enemy clutches, but somehow I'd managed to keep it safe . . .

I had carried the egg with me for a whole day when it started to rattle and shake. From the scratching sounds coming from inside, I knew it was probably ready to hatch! When a little dragon's face popped out from the top of the egg, it suddenly struck me – I now had a baby dragon to take care of. What on earth do you do with a dragon?

I named him Colin. It didn't seem like a good idea to keep an energetic little pet around while on an important mission, but I couldn't exactly leave him behind either. He was too small to fend for himself in the wilderness, and even if I tried to set him free, he refused to leave my side.

Wherever I went, he was there in the grass, hopping along beside me, wagging his little tail. He was with me when I collected the supplies I'd been sent to fetch from the Bin Weevil base, and he came with me when I made the return journey back through the mountains to bring the supplies back to my friends.

We'd come almost all the way back to the Bin Weevil camp where I was meant to meet my friends, when trouble struck – I tripped an enemy trap. I fell into a shallow pit and dropped my pack. *Snap!* went a twig under my foot, and *whoosh!* went a big rope net as it fell down from a tree and entangled me. I was stuck. I couldn't reach my pack, and I didn't have anything with which to cut the net.

I knew the enemy would be coming soon, and if they found me, I was doomed. Worse still, little Colin could fall into their clutches. 'Run away!' I told him. 'Colin, please run away!' But he didn't understand, he just wanted to stay beside me.

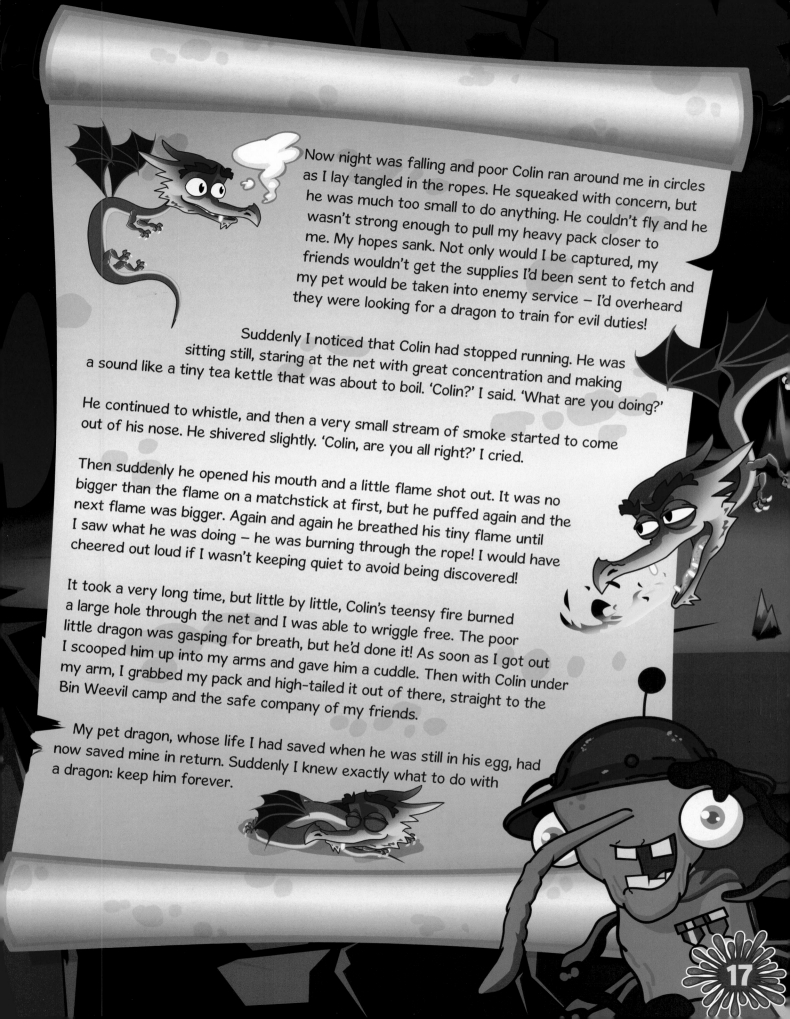

Now night was falling and poor Colin ran around me in circles as I lay tangled in the ropes. He squeaked with concern, but he was much too small to do anything. He couldn't fly and he wasn't strong enough to pull my heavy pack closer to me. My hopes sank. Not only would I be captured, my friends wouldn't get the supplies I'd been sent to fetch and my pet would be taken into enemy service – I'd overheard they were looking for a dragon to train for evil duties!

Suddenly I noticed that Colin had stopped running. He was sitting still, staring at the net with great concentration and making a sound like a tiny tea kettle that was about to boil. 'Colin?' I said. 'What are you doing?'

He continued to whistle, and then a very small stream of smoke started to come out of his nose. He shivered slightly. 'Colin, are you all right?' I cried.

Then suddenly he opened his mouth and a little flame shot out. It was no bigger than the flame on a matchstick at first, but he puffed again and the next flame was bigger. Again and again he breathed his tiny flame until I saw what he was doing – he was burning through the rope! I would have cheered out loud if I wasn't keeping quiet to avoid being discovered!

It took a very long time, but little by little, Colin's teensy fire burned a large hole through the net and I was able to wriggle free. The poor little dragon was gasping for breath, but he'd done it! As soon as I got out I scooped him up into my arms and gave him a cuddle. Then with Colin under my arm, I grabbed my pack and high-tailed it out of there, straight to the Bin Weevil camp and the safe company of my friends.

My pet dragon, whose life I had saved when he was still in his egg, had now saved mine in return. Suddenly I knew exactly what to do with a dragon: keep him forever.

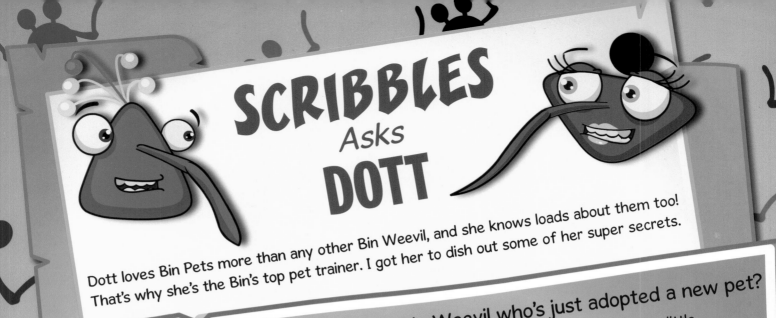

SCRIBBLES
Asks
DOTT

Dott loves Bin Pets more than any other Bin Weevil, and she knows loads about them too! That's why she's the Bin's top pet trainer. I got her to dish out some of her super secrets.

Dott, can you share any good advice for a Bin Weevil who's just adopted a new pet?

Well, you'll need to get to know each other, so spend a lot of time together! Your pet might be a little shy when first arriving home, and it will take some time for your pet to start exploring. Place your Bin Pet's bed and bowl in the same room at first to make it easy for your pet to find their things.

What should you do if your pet doesn't look happy?

Your pet could be tired or hungry, so check their energy and food levels to see what might be the matter. If your pet is fed and rested but is still acting a little grouchy, try a few strokes – he or she might just want some attention from you!

Bin Pets love to play together when they meet. What's the best way to get your Bin Pet to meet new playmates?

Flum's Fountain is a great place to meet other Bin Pet owners, so you can usually find some playmates for your pet there. But if your pet doesn't want to go out, why not try inviting a Bin Buddy over and ask them to bring their Bin Pet along? Your pets will play together inside the nest as well as outside.

DOODLE LOVES TO DANCE, ESPECIALLY TO THE BIN PETS BOP!

Bin Pets aren't just cute, they're clever too! Read on for some of my top tips on how to train them!

DOTT'S TOP TRAINING TIPS

Make sure your Bin Pet is not tired or hungry when you start to play. Pets usually love to learn new tricks, but if they're not feeling up to it, they can get quite grumpy when you ask them to play. It's best to wait until your pet is well fed, well rested and has a high energy level to get the best results from your training.

Before learning to juggle, your Bin Pet will first need to learn the 'fetch' and 'throw to me' commands. Practise these tricks with your pet daily, and don't forget to reward your pet with a stroke when they get it right!

When the 'juggle' command shows up in your Bin Pet's actions menu, your pet is now ready to learn the coolest tricks of all! To start your pet's juggling lesson, first ask your pet to sit and stay. Then, throw the ball over to your pet and ask it to juggle by clicking the 'juggle' action.

At first, your Bin Pet might not be very good at juggling. When your pet drops a ball and doesn't look happy, give some encouragement by stroking your pet before using the juggle command again. We all make mistakes and practice makes perfect!

The more often your pet juggles, the faster new skills will come and the more juggling tricks will appear in your pet's actions menu. With lots of practice, your pet can learn to juggle up to nine balls! Wow!

BIN STYLE

POSH

Bin Style: Sparkly, elegant and totally on trend

Top accessory: Jewelled tiara

What this look says: I'm the first one to be seen showing off a new style, because I probably set it myself. I always plan my outfits — even if I'm just eating toast in my pyjamas, they're totally coordinated with my slippers.

PUNT

Bin Style: Upper-crust, classic and refined

Top accessory: Jaunty cap

What this look says: I'm a weevily gent who takes his fashion seriously. You won't catch me without my gold watch and my clothes are always perfectly pressed! I dress to impress no matter what I'm doing.

WIGG

Bin Style: Bright, kooky and off-the-wall

Top accessory: Colourful hairpiece

What this look says: I'm a trailblazing individual and I'm not afraid to look a bit different! Big, bold patterns and crazy colours don't scare me off — in fact, I love 'em!

Bin Style:

Top accessory:

What this look says:

ME

20

DID YOU KNOW?

Someone who makes fancy hats is called a milliner and the art of making hats is called millinery!

Greetings, I'm Hem! Tong's great at putting together a look, and I'm the designer behind some of the Bin's top fashions. Not only did I sew Fling's super-famous disco suit, I also made Tink's unique waistcoat! I love to make clothes, but hats are my speciality I lurrve selling them at my boutique, Hem's Hats.

Recognize these Bin-tastic hats? I made them all! Can you match each one to the right owner? (Sneaky hint: Check out the photos on pages 50–53!)

I managed to catch up with the Bin's busiest builder as he rushed from one construction site to the next. I asked him ten seriously rapid-fire questions, so he could answer between bites of the Slime Sandwich he was eating on the go!

SCRIBBLES
Asks
RIGG

Cooking or Dining Out?
Who has time to cook with a schedule like mine? I keep Figg's and Tum's in business.

Track Builder or Track Tester?
Track Builder for sure! I'm a builder by trade, so let's leave the testing to the racers!

Slime Sandwich or Bin Burger?

Dosh's Palace or Rigg's Multiplex?
Hey now! Rigg's may have my name on it, but I built Dosh's Palace and it's one of my finest masterpieces. I refuse to choose.

Mulch Coins or Dosh Coins?
I prefer the nice, gooey Mulch coin. As a builder I do appreciate a little grime!

Statues or Fountains?
What about a fountain with a statue in the middle? Want me to build you one? Problem solved!

SWS Headquarters or Lab's Lab?
Definitely SWS HQ! I don't think Lab's is structurally sound. The HQ on the other hand, is an unbreakable stronghold. Did I mention I built it?

Munch Bug or Tonk?
Tonk! Those critters are strong workers. If only they weren't microscopic, I could use some of those tough tortoises on my building sites.

Bin-jitsu or the Bin Weevils Dance?
I'm not much of a dancer, but I know a few Bin-jitsu moves. Kong Fu taught them to me while I was renovating the Special Ops Training Room!

Tink or Clott?
ARRRGH! Did you have to mention those two? Crikey! I've really got to dash before they get my bulldozer stuck in the Slime Pool again!

QUIZ: WHICH HOME IS FOR YOU?

From weird to wacky to gorgeous and glamorous, I built all the Bin's most famous homes. Take the quiz to find out which famous Bin Weevil's home you'd most like to live in!

It's important to live somewhere that's suited to your hobbies. What do you do in the evenings to relax?
A) I count up all my Mulch in a huge vault.
B) I do a crossword or read by the fireplace.
C) I work on the cool gadget I've been building.

What kinds of guests do you expect to entertain once you've moved into your new home?
A) Only the upper crust for me – my friends are all VIPs!
B) My buddies are mostly artists, poets and creative types.
C) Mad scientists . . . and maybe a Frankenweevil or two.

Where would you bring a party of guests when they first arrive?
A) Into the grand hall, to show them the architecture.
B) Into the library, to show them my newest book.
C) Into the laboratory, to show them my latest invention!

What's the most unusual feature in your dream home?
A) It has loads of secret passageways and hidden vaults.
B) It's haunted, so it comes with a few eccentric ghosts!
C) It's got lots of zany contraptions and gadgets inside!

MOSTLY As:
DOSH'S PALACE
The wealthiest and most elegant Bin Weevil siblings inhabit the fanciest abode in the Binscape. Everything is gilded and glittering! You'd love to move in with Dosh and Posh, living it up in luxury and counting your piles of Mulch.

MOSTLY Bs:
FLEM MANOR
Bookish Flem needs lots of room for his library and word puzzles . . . and, of course, lots of fine furniture for the ghosts to move around! You'd be right at home in his comfy study with a cup of hot Scent Flower Tea.

MOSTLY Cs:
LAB'S LAB
Mad inventors need a home built with extra-strong materials, because you never know when a kooky contraption might go wild! You're a brainiac who'd love living in Lab's Lab, surrounded by gadgets and totally cool science!

23

SILLY STORIES

How to play Silly Stories

Write a short story, leaving some of the words blank!
Ask a friend to help you fill the spaces . . . but your pal
won't get to see the whole story until afterwards.
You'll end up with a super-silly tale!

STEP 1

Write your story, replacing some of the words with a blank space. Under each blank, write down the type of word that should fill the space. If you need an action word then write 'VERB' under it, if you need a descriptive word write 'ADJECTIVE', and so on.

STEP 2

Take a separate sheet of paper and write the word types you need along the left side. Give the list to your buddy and ask them to write the first thing that came to mind beside each type of word.

STEP 3

Read your story out loud, filling in your friend's words along the way! Tip: you can play with a group of friends by taking it in turns to add words. Or you could make a 'silly word sack' and fill a bag with cards containing words of each type, then draw them at random!

Here are some word types you might need:

CHARACTER / PLACE / OBJECT

Examples: flower, Bin Pet, fountain, Bunty
Tell your friend which type of noun you need.
You could even be more specific, for example
'type of pet', but it's best to leave it to your
friend's imagination. The less info they have,
the funnier your story will be!

ADJECTIVE

Examples: tiny, blue, heavy, funny
A descriptive word that tells you more about an object. It could be a colour, a size or a word that tells you what something looks like.

VERB

Examples: run, spin, juggle, dance
An action word that tells you what someone is doing.

24

ADVERB

Examples: slowly, clumsily, brilliantly, excitedly
Add 'ly' to the end of an adjective to describe the way that someone did something!

Here are some more word types you might need:

EXCLAMATION

Examples: Bin-tastic! Yikes! Hey! Whoa!
A shout or an expression that a character could yell out.

Check it out!

I played the Silly Stories game with Tink and this is what he came up with. Read my story and use Tink's words when you come to a blank. That Bin-brain of his sure is full of crazy ideas!

One day, I was at _____ when I lost my _____ hat. I looked
              place   adjective

everywhere, even underneath the _____ and beside the_____ but
                                   object   object

I couldn't find it. I couldn't keep looking because it was time to go and walk my

_____. Suddenly, just as I was _____ stopping to buy a _____ to eat,
animal   adverb   object

I noticed my friend_____in the queue in front of me. '_____!'
                  name   exclamation

I shouted. 'Have you seen my_____?' My buddy replied, 'No, but I just _____
                            object   past tense verb

a new _____ and now I'm ready to _____!'
        object   verb

Tink's List

Place: Flum's Fountain

Adjective: smelly

Object: cannonball

Object: bathtub

Animal: koala

Adverb: calmly

Object: Scent Flower

Name: Posh

Exclamation: Jeepers!

Object: stapler

Past tense verb: painted

Object: trombone

Verb: swim

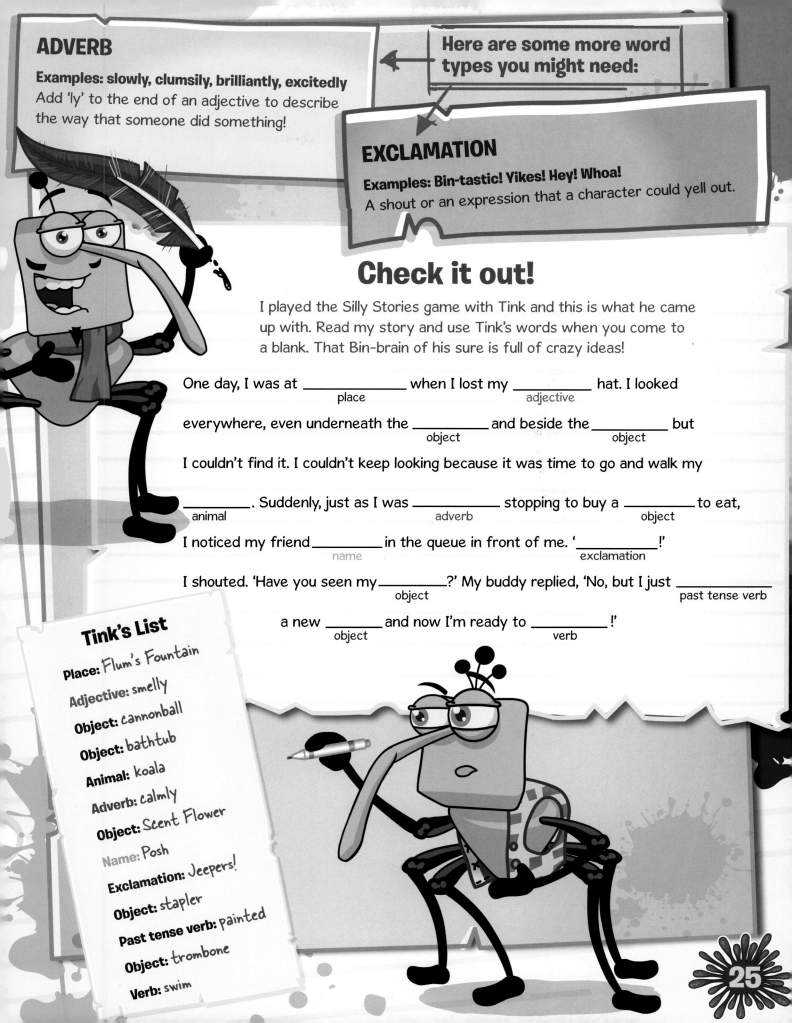

DIRT VALLEY MAZE

Zip is on course to beat Ham's Binspeed record, but this track is weevily tough! Help Zip avoid the obstacles and pick up all the racing flags on her way to the finish line!

HAM

Autograph: Ham

Car number: 2

Claim to fame: Has won more weevily racing trophies than any other racer.

Speed secret: Skidding around tricky corners like a whizz!

Favourite kind of track: Lots of twists and turns . . . and hazards!

Fave pre-race snack: Fruit smoothie

Fun fact: He once lost a wheel during a race and still came first!

ZIP

Autograph: Zip

Car number: 8

Claim to fame: Beat the Binspeed record in a custom-built car.

Speed secret: Turbo-acceleration and a super-powered engine!

Favourite kind of track: Long stretches of open road to build up speed.

Fave pre-race snack: Dirt Doughnut

Fun fact: Her car number is 8 because it's Lab's favourite number and he helped build her amazing hyperspeed engine.

Cone Confusion

Yum, yum! It's ice-cream time on the beach! Can you match each Bin Weevil to the ice-cream cone that they bought?

Posh and Tink have the same number of scoops.

Both Bunty and Posh have a vanilla scoop on the top of their cone.

Clott ordered one scoop of each flavour!

Did You Know?

The Ice-Cream Machine on Mulch Island was built right on top of an ancient underground temple! Rigg discovered the entrance right in the spot where he'd planned to put the Ice-Cream Machine at first, so he had to move the construction a little to the left to avoid disturbing the ancient site. Of course, Digg was no help at all for the rest of the project – he was too busy nosing around in the temple and investigating the archaeological findings to help Rigg! That's why Rigg had to call Tink and Clott in to help him install the Ice-Cream Machine . . . let's just say that was an ex-*cream*-ly bad idea!

28

Wild for Wildlife

Mulch Island and the archipelago surrounding it are home to lots of strange plants and creatures! Keen photographer Snappy loves to take a flight out to the island to get some Bin-tastic wildlife photos. Check out some of her latest shots.

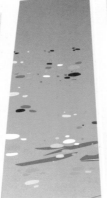

The largest fish ever to splash in the Mulch Island Ocean can be seriously hard to catch on camera! Imagine Snappy's delight when she landed this amazing close-up!

These unusual creatures don't move very much – in fact, the first explorers on Mulch Island mistook them for green rocks! They love to sun themselves near the water, but they don't venture very far from their favourite spot.

Something about the warm, humid climate on Mulch Island makes Scent Flowers grow to an enormous size! Just don't get caught in their spray – you'll be absolutely drenched in smelly vapour.

The trees around the Bin Pet Temple are dotted with lots of these sticky fly nests, which can make things really unpleasant for jungle trekkers! These flies are hardly ever spotted on the mainland, except at Tink's Tree.

The Mulch Island millipedes might give you a fright as they dart out of the shadows, but they're completely harmless. They like to feed on the orange berries found deeper in the jungle.

29

LAB

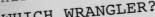

Speciality: Inventions
Inspired by his hero, Slosh, Lab has been inventing things for as long as he can remember. Most of the gadgets he builds have an uncanny tendency to go out of control . . . so it's a good thing most of his lab now has self-rebuilding walls!

WHICH WRANGLER?
Two of these prototypes for the Venus Flytrap Wrangler are the same. Can you find which ones are exactly alike?

A B C D E F

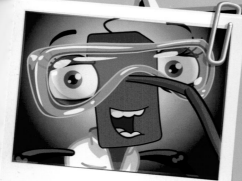

KEM

Speciality: Potions
Safety-conscious Kem tries to keep the lab in order and makes sure everyone is wearing goggles when doing experiments. Too bad she can't keep Lab's inventions in check!

TEST TUBE TIZZY
Kem had 20 empty test tubes on her shelf this morning. She filled 1/4 of them with potions by midday, then filled twice as many in the afternoon. In the evening, she made 3 more potions. How many empty tubes did she have left at the end of the day?

Fill these with bubbling potions in weird and wacky colours!

Speciality: Mathematics
Dedicated Sum is always working out problems, even in her sleep! She's also one of the top codebreakers for the Secret Weevil Service.

SLIPPERY SUMS
Some of the numbers in Sum's equations have slipped out of place. Can you put them back where they belong?

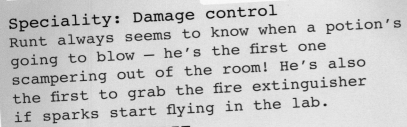

$$(6 \times \underline{\quad}) + 13 = 49$$
$$(16 - \underline{\quad}) \times 3 = 24$$
$$15 - (2 \times 5) = \underline{\quad}$$
$$(10 - 8) \times \underline{\quad} = 6$$

6

8

3   5

RUNT

Speciality: Damage control
Runt always seems to know when a potion's going to blow — he's the first one scampering out of the room! He's also the first to grab the fire extinguisher if sparks start flying in the lab.

PUZZLING PORTRAIT
Eek! When Lab accidentally set off the Mulch Cannon indoors again, this portrait of Great-Uncle Slosh fell off the wall and shattered. Can you help Runt put the missing pieces back in place?

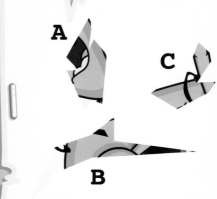

A

C

B

BIN BOTS WORKSHOP

The first Bin Bots were created by chanc
when a mishap with a shrink ray caused
havoc in Lab's Lab! They turned out to be
Lab's most brilliant creation and many mor
wacky and wonderful bots have followed.
Check out the sketches of some of these
Bin-tastic bots!

Hamma Bird

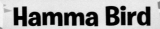

These beaky bots are taller than they
seem – just check out those cool extendable
legs that let Hamma Bird tower over the
others! Such bendy limbs come in really handy for breakdancing.

Snuffle Be

Don't be frightened of this buzzy critter – Snuffle
Bees have no sting in their tails! Their weird funnel-
shaped snouts let them pick up objects with a
vacuum-like suction. How *buzz*-arre!

Rockilla

Ooh, someone's angry! These rock-busting
grouches just can't keep their rage in check.
When they lose their cool, they can smash
through stone with those chunky fists.

Whoa! Check out these zany doodles! Could these be some of Lab's top-secret ideas for new Bin Bots? What do you think these Bin Bots will be called? Write a cool name for each bot beside the sketch!

ARE YOU A BIN BOT ENGINEER?

Bin Bots are all different! Some are cute and fuzzy, some are total oddballs and some look tough or even a little scary! Draw your own sketch for a new Bin Bot here. What will your bot's special skills be?

HOW TO DRAW WINK

Hello, me hearties! I'm Wink – Bin pirate, treasure hunter and adventurer! When I'm not busy sailing the seven seas in search of sparkly treasure, I'm quite the arrr-tist! I love drawing pictures of me Bin Maties. If you'd like to draw me, then follow these simple steps to create me piraty portrait. Shiver me timbers!

TOP TIP:
Sketch very lightly with a pencil at first. If you make a mistake, you can always rub it out. Some parts of your drawing will need to be sketched over the top of others too. You can trace over your finished lines with a darker line later!

1 To start, draw a square shape for Wink's head, overlapping a triangle with rounded corners for the body.

2 Draw a line down and another across the middle of the head. This will help you to position the eyes and nose. Next, draw two circles for the eyes and two thin sausage shapes for the nose, ending the second one in a point.

3 For each arm and leg, draw two sausage shapes, one short and squat and one longer and thinner. Remember to leave a space for Wink's peg leg!

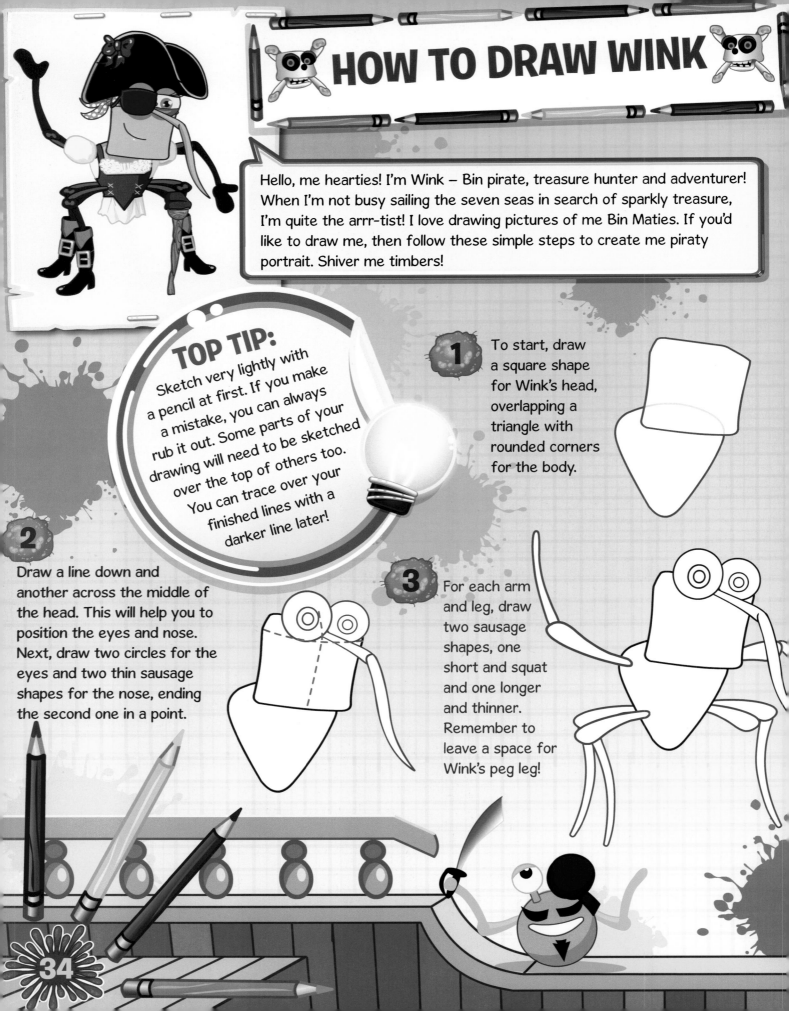

w an oval shape
each hand, then
the thumbs. You
add an outline to
shapes when
've finished.

5 Add some squashed circles for Wink's elbows and knees.

6 Next, add Wink's dress, boots and peg leg. Don't forget the details, like the creases, buckles, ruffles and stitches.

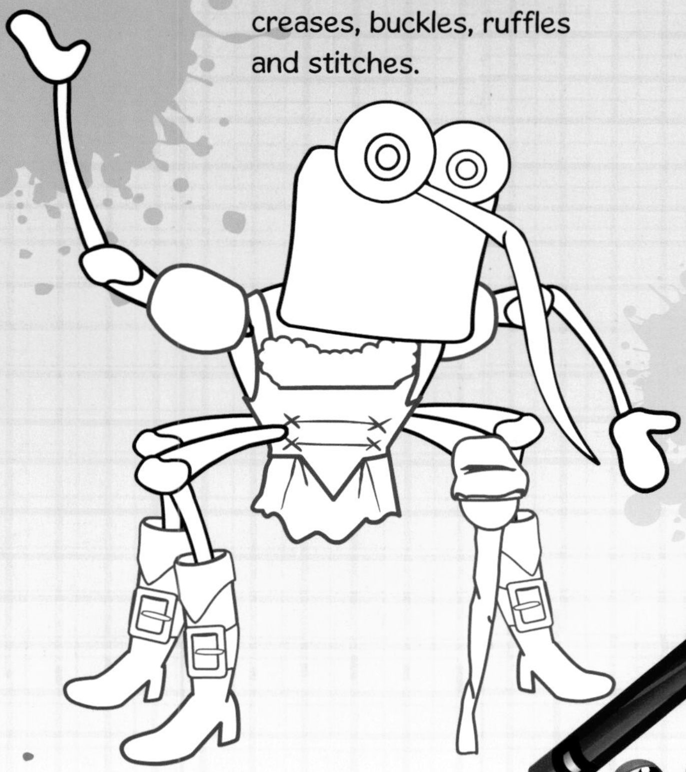

7 Draw Wink's mouth, eyelashes, eyebrows and eye patch. Finish by adding her big pirate hat and bandana. Finally, follow the outline of your drawing with a thin marker or pen, then rub out any extra pencil lines before colouring Wink in!

TREASURE HUNTERS

Weevily treasure hunters Wink and Gem are always competing – they both want to be first to get their feelers on the treasure! They've just uncovered a massive haul of loot at the same time and they're racing to pick it all up as fast as they can.

Use the map, the compass and the directions to follow the route each treasure hunter took. Find out who collected the most Mulch coins, who found the most jewels and who scooped up that mysterious treasure chest!

WINK'S ROUTE

Start: W
3 North
2 East
2 North
1 East
2 South
2 East

GEM'S ROUTE

Start: G
3 South
2 West
1 South
1 East
1 South
2 West

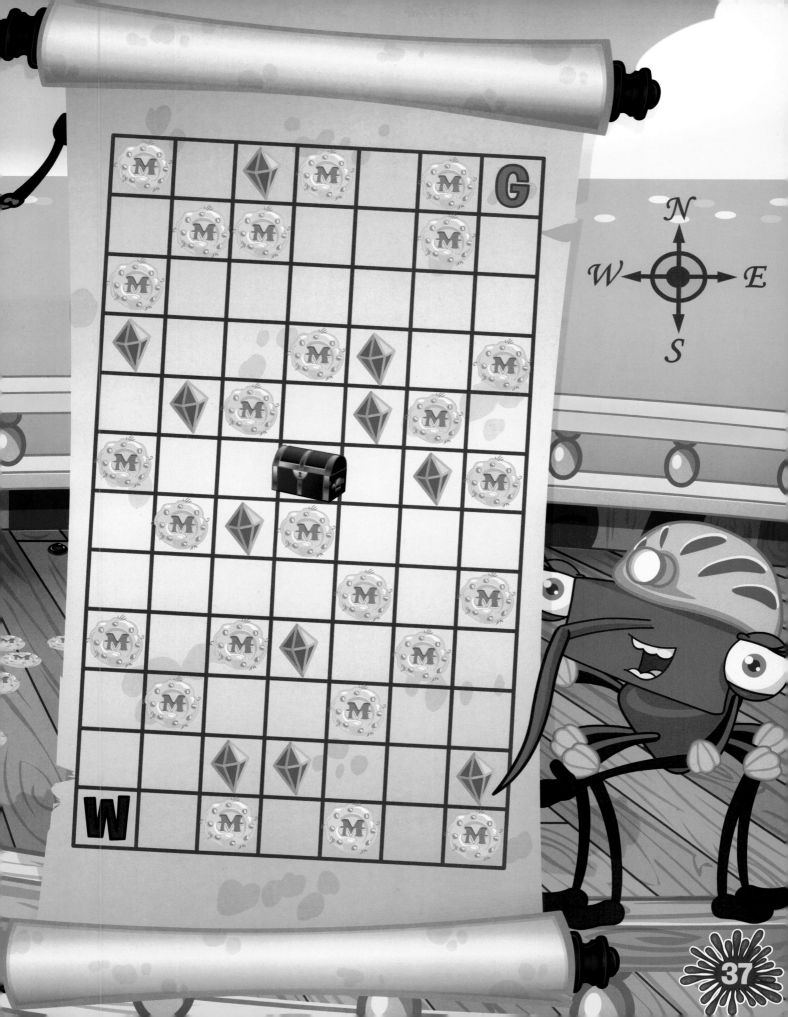

MAKE A SCENT FLOWER

YOUNGER BIN WEEVILS, PLEASE ASK A PARENT TO HELP WITH CUTTING OUT!

You will need:

A pencil
Some old newspaper
Coloured thin card or craft foam
Glue or tape
Scissors
White acrylic paint
A small thin paintbrush
Pipe cleaners
A ball of modelling clay

STEP 1. Use your pencil to draw a flat flower shape on your coloured card and carefully cut it out. Make sure you don't cut your petals too close together because you'll need to leave some room in the centre of your flower. (Don't worry if all the petals aren't exactly the same size – after all, each flower is unique!)

STEP 2. Roll a small square piece of card into a cone shape. Roll it as thin as possible at the pointy end. Once you're happy with the shape of your cone, secure it in place with tape or glue, then trim around the wide edge until it's nice and even.

STEP 3. Time to add the stripes! Cover your working surface with piece of old newspaper to protec it before you paint. Balance the cone on its wide edge and hold t top with your finger while you pa some white stripes around it. Th might take some time to dry, so patient! (You could also try gluing thin strips of white paper to mak the stripes a different way!)

STEP 4. Poke a hole through the centre of your flat flower shape using your pencil. The hole should be about the width of the pencil, or a little larger depending on the size of your cone. Push the thin end of the cone through the hole and secure the two pieces together at the back with a small piece of tape.

STEP 5. Tape a pipe cleaner securely to the back of your scent flower, checking you can hold up your flower by the stem. If your flower doesn't stand up very well, try twisting two pipe cleaners together to make the stem stronger. Hint: use very thin paper or craft foam to make the head of your flower, rather than thick card. The lighter the material, the straighter your flower will stand!

STEP 6. To hide all that messy tape where the pieces are joined together, take some thin strips of green tissue paper and glue them around the back of the flower, carefully covering the part where the stem and the flower head meet.

STEP 7. Finish off your flower with some leaves cut from green paper. Again you can glue some tissue paper around the stem to cover the tape where they're attached.

STEP 8. Plant your flower! To make your flower stand up, stick the stem into a small lump of modelling clay that you've moulded into a flowerpot shape. You could even make a vase out of a recycled juice bottle!

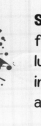

GET CREATIVE!

Now that you know how to make a Scent Flower, why not have a go at making some other types of flowers to fill up your Bin Garden? Try making up some wacky flowers of your own! Send a snap of your flowers or other crafts to **pics@binweevils.com** and you could be featured on our Fan Art Page!

OCTEELIA

TOP SECRET

MEMO TO: ELITE SWS AGENTS
STATUS: EXTREMELY URGENT
SUBJECT: SPIDERS!

Spiders were last seen in the Bin during the Great Bin War. We thought they were gone forever. But it seems they may have been lurking in the shadows, watching and waiting for a chance to strike. A spider named **OCTEELIA** is at the head of the organization known as the WEB — or Weevil Extermination Bureau. Are there more of them out there? Are we prepared if there are?

We know that the Bin Weevil Changer has been used to create many evil clones of that twisted Bin Weevil known as **THUGG**. We also know that Octeelia has been successful in disguising herself as a Bin Weevil named **LIA**. So far, it has not been possible for our enemy to use the Bin Weevil Changer technology to turn Bin Weevils into spiders . . . but intelligence suggests that this may be their current objective. This must NOT be allowed to happen while the Secret Weevil Service stand watch.

Agents, be extremely vigilant. The WEB menace must be contained!

PLEASE DESTROY THIS
MESSAGE AFTER READING.

THUGG

LIA

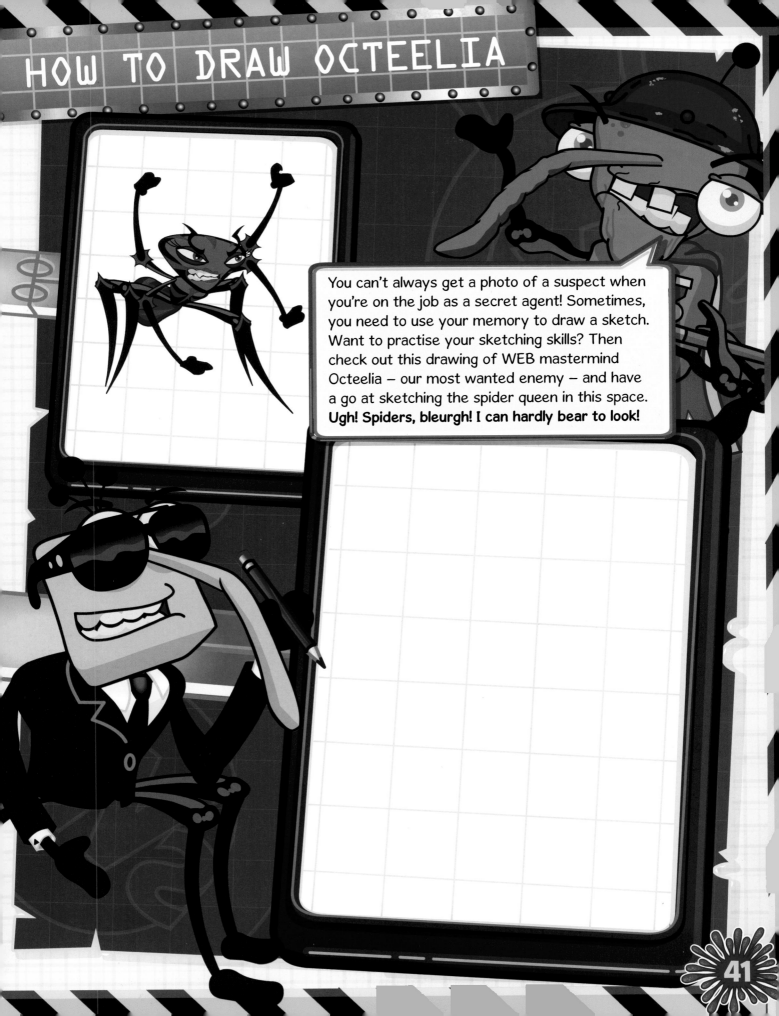

You can't always get a photo of a suspect when you're on the job as a secret agent! Sometimes, you need to use your memory to draw a sketch. Want to practise your sketching skills? Then check out this drawing of WEB mastermind Octeelia – our most wanted enemy – and have a go at sketching the spider queen in this space. **Ugh! Spiders, bleurgh! I can hardly bear to look!**

BE WEEVILY GREEN!

Hey! I'm Pong, the greenest Bin Weevil in the Bin. What? Yeah, of course I know I'm red – I meant green as in ENVIRONMENTALLY FRIENDLY. Come on!

As I was saying . . . I love to recycle, so I'm always on the lookout for unusual objects that other Bin Weevils have thrown away. Here are some ideas for recycling objects you find around the house into cool and useful stuff!

A TIN CAN

could become a holder for your pens, pencils or markers! Choose one with no jagged edges and wash it carefully. You can decorate the outside with stickers, paint or glitter!

OLD COMICS PAGES

can be used to make quirky and cool wrapping paper! After your buddy opens their gift, they can read the wrapping!

AN EMPTY TISSUE BOX

could become a great storage container for your Bin Weevils trading cards. Cut dividers out of cardboard to help you sort your cards with your own special filing system!

A PLASTIC CONTAINER

can become a cool miniature planter for a seedling! Carefully poke a couple of holes in the bottom and place the container on to a plate. Fill it with potting soil and place a seed inside. Follow the instructions on the seed packet to give your plant the right amount of light and water, then watch it grow! When it's big enough, you could even plant your seedling outside.

LIDS FROM PLASTIC BOTTLES

make great game tokens if you're making up your own board game. Add a sticker to the top to personalize your token!

44

YOUNGER BIN WEEVILS: PLEASE ASK A PARENT FOR HELP WHEN USING SCISSORS OR HANDLING SHARP MATERIALS.

MAKE A WEEVILY BIN!

Got a boring old bin in your room?

Got some old mags you've finished reading? You're just a few steps away from a pop art masterpiece!

You will need:

- small metal or plastic rubbish bin
- some old newspaper
- magazine clippings (small, colourful images work best)
- PVA glue
- stickers or glitter
- scissors
- a large paintbrush
- plastic containers or trays (the recycling bin is a great place to look for these!)
- spray glue (OPTIONAL)

YOUNGER BIN WEEVILS, PLEASE ASK A PARENT TO HELP WITH CUTTING OUT!

PREPARATION:
Cut out all the pictures that you want to use and place them within easy reach. (We used some old Bin Weevils magazines!) Cover your work surface with newspaper. Pour some glue into one plastic container and a little bit of water into the other.

STEP 1. Use your brush to spread a thin layer of glue over one section of your bin, then start sticking your magazine clippings. Don't worry about the pictures being straight – it will actually look better if they're a bit random! HINT: It's best to work on one section at a time, so your glue doesn't dry out while you work.

STEP 2. When you've finished a section, dip your brush in the water and gently dab over all the positioned clippings. Do this until the edges of the pictures are all lying flat. (Don't use too much water, or your pics might go wrinkly!)

STEP 3. Continue all the way around, then go around again to cover any bare spaces. It's fine to layer one picture on top of another! Remember to use your water and glue each time you place new pictures and dab down your edges.

STEP 4. When you've finished, leave your bin until everything is completely dry. It should have a nice shine to it when the glue has dried! Now you can add some stickers or glitter to finish off your design. If you really want your bin to last a long time, glaze over the entire surface with a thin coating of spray glue to seal it. (Ask a grown-up for help and only use spray glue in a well-ventilated room or outdoors.)

SCRIBBLES Asks POSH

Stylish Posh likes the finer things in life, and her sophisticated Bin Pet, Lady Wawa, gets nothing less than the best! From golden food bowls to her own miniature Bin Pet Palace, Lady Wawa has it all. I had a word with Posh about life with the Bin's most pampered pet . . . read on!

Posh, how did you pick out your Bin Pet?

I guess you could say she chose me! I popped into the Bin Pet Shop with my brother, Dosh, for a browse. Lady Wawa came running right up to me. She was so cute! I just had to adopt her and we've been inseparable ever since. Dosh was a bit annoyed, as we had to carry her home inside his top hat!

Does Dosh get along with Lady Wawa now?

Oh, he has his grouchy moments with her . . . like when she dug up his prize Scent Flower, or that time she chewed his favourite gold-tipped walking stick! But secretly I think he adores her almost as much as I do.

How did you feel when Lady Wawa was kidnapped by the WEB?

Oh! I was devastated! What a horrible thing to happen! I was so worried about my precious little Wawakins, I couldn't stop crying . . . but I knew that the SWS could find her. They're so brave! They brought her back to me safe and sound.

What's your Bin Pet's top skill?

Lady Wawa is an amazing juggler. She makes me so proud. I always bring her juggling balls with me wherever we go so she can show off.

READY TO PLAY

LADY WAWA FACT FILE

Talented Lady Wawa is an amazing juggler and can throw her juggling balls almost as high as the roof of Dosh's Palace!

Her favourite place in the Binscape is Flum's Fountain – it's the best spot to show off her tricks!

Lady Wawa prefers to have her food bowl presented on a pink cushion.

Her favourite snack is Bin Pet Treats that are shaped like hearts – Posh has these specially imported for her.

Lady Wawa became the Bin's most famous Bin Pet when she was kidnapped by Weevil X. Luckily, she was rescued by the SWS!

Lady Wawa's favourite playmate is Scribbles' Bin Pet, Doodle. They have a great time whenever Scribbles comes by to interview Posh!

SOOOO CUTE!

DINNER TIME!

TUCKERED OUT

CHAMPION JUGGLER

PET-NAPPED!

RACING RIDDLE

Zip and Ham have taken a day off from the racetrack, leaving a spot open for a brand-new Weevil Wheels Champion to bag a trophy! Scribbles has written a report about what happened during the race, but his notes have got mixed up! Can you work out who won the race, and how long each racer took to complete the course?

Stunt   Trigg   Dip   Bing   Fab

Stunt, Trigg, Dip, Bing and Fab started the race.

The winning racer completed the course in just 60 seconds!

Bing was 7 seconds slower than the winner.

Dip finished the race 3 seconds after Bing, but 4 seconds ahead of Fab.

Bing and Trigg finished the race tied in second place.

Draw a picture of the winning racer and their gold trophy here!

PHOTO FINISH

Eagle-eyed Hunt has spotted some strange differences between these pictures of the photo finish at the Weevil Wheels racetrack last week! That super-sleuth doesn't miss a thing! Can you spot the ten differences between the original photo and the copy below?

ORIGINAL

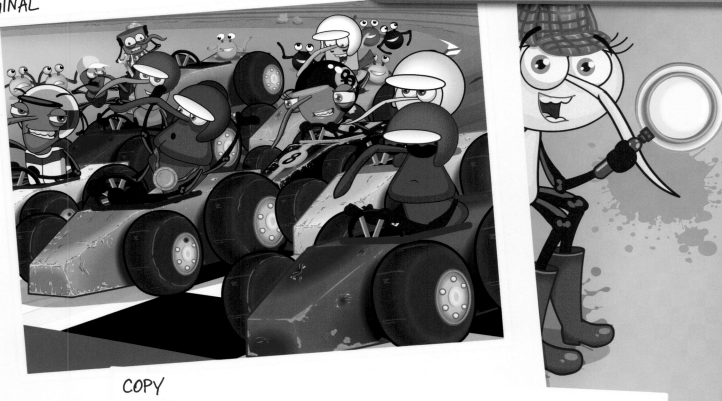

COPY

49

FAMILY ALBUM

DOSH FAMILY

GAM FAMILY

TUM FAMILY

ROTT FAMILY

INK FAMILY

KIP FAMILY

BING FAMILY

FAMILY ALBUM

TAB FAMILY

GONG FAMILY

PUNT FAMILY

RIGG FAMILY

FLEM FAMILY

SPECIAL BIN FRIENDS

ME AND MY BUDDIES

Draw yourself and your friends in the space above.

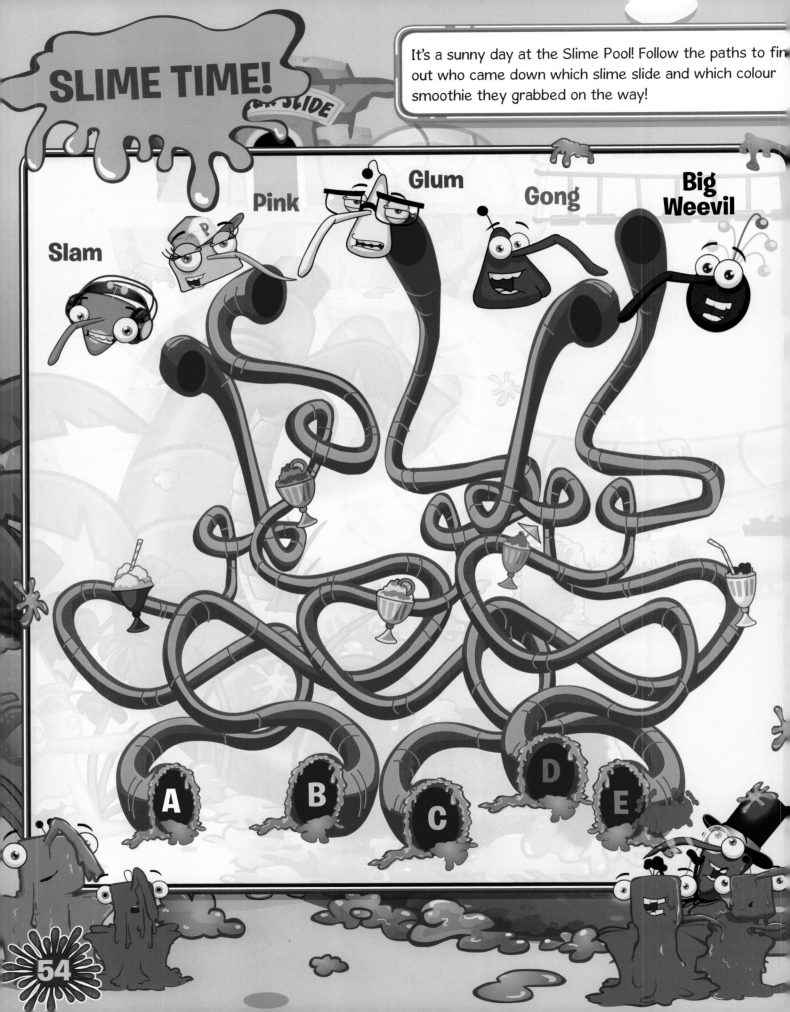

It's always summertime at the Slime Pool. Balmy beaches lapped by slimy green waves – what could be more relaxing? Can you place all these summertime words into the grid where they belong? We've popped a few letters into place to help you along.

3 LETTERS
SUN ☐
HOT ☐

4 LETTERS
SAND ☐
WARM ☐
POOL ☐
PALM ☐

5 LETTERS
BEACH ☐
SLIME ☐
RELAX ☐

6 LETTERS
BREEZY ☐
SPLASH ☐

7 LETTERS
HOLIDAY ☐
FRIENDS ☐

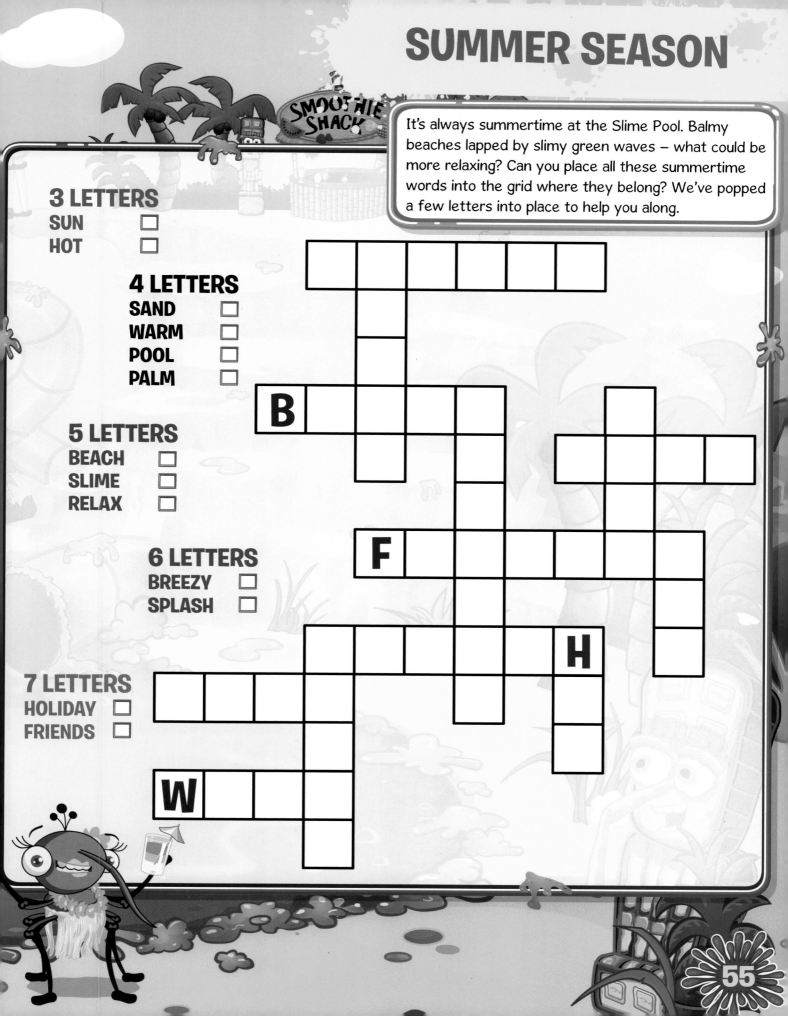

BIN BATTLE GAME

The SWS and the WEB are going head to head in an epic Bin battle! Grab a buddy then flip a coin to decide who will be who. Whose tactics will come out on top?

HOW TO PLAY:

Carefully cut along the lines, then give two battle grids to each player. Use one grid to position your own pieces on and one grid to keep track of where your opponent's pieces are.

First, draw each of your six pieces anywhere you like on your own grid. (To see what the pieces look like and how many spaces they should take up, check out the Target Shapes & Sizes.) Make sure your opponent can't see your grid!

Now take turns throwing a water balloon to see if you can strike an enemy target! To throw a water balloon, call out the grid coordinates where your balloon has landed (e.g. 'I throw to A6!')

If the other player 'hits' a square where you've got a piece, you must shout 'Hit!'. If there's nothing in the square they chose, it's a miss — give your best evil cackle if you're the WEB player, and shout 'Not so fast, Weevil X!' if you're the SWS player!

When you land a hit on your opponent, colour in the square so you can remember where it is. If you've called out a square that doesn't have anything on it, draw an X in that square to remind you not to call it out again. Once you've landed a hit, try to guess which piece it might be and figure out which other squares it occupies! (When all the squares occupied by a piece have been hit, that piece goes out of play.)

The winner is the first player to take all enemy pieces out of play. **Victory!**

TARGET SHAPES & SIZES

1 x Giant Laser = 4 Squares

2 x Agent/Thugg = 2 Squares

2 x Control Point = 3 Squares

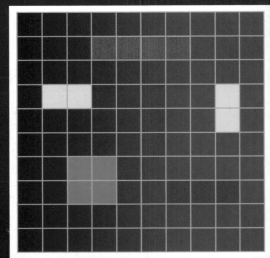

1 x Base = 4 Squares

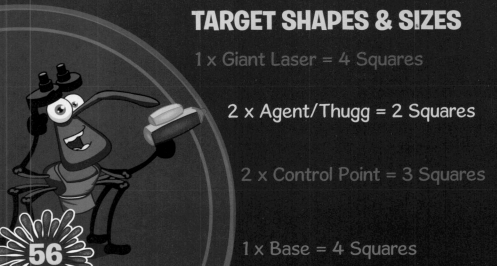

HINT: Ask a parent to photocopy this page if you'd like to play the game again and again.

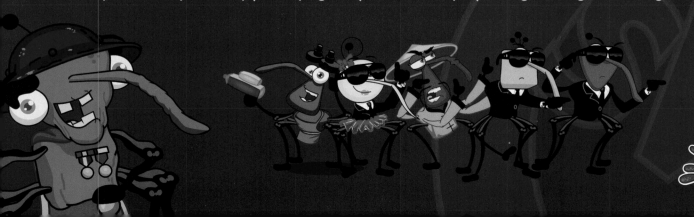

Top codebreaker Sum has been urgently summoned to S
Headquarters! The SWS have intercepted a coded messa
written by Octeelia and they need Sum's help to crack it!

TOP SECRET

CODE KEY

$G = 3 \times 3$

$S = 21 \div 3$

$M = (5 \times 3) - 15$

$R = (6 - 2) \times 2$

$D = (18 \div 6) - 2$

$E = 5 \times 2$

$L = (20 \div 2) - 8$

$O = 8 \div 2$

$T = (12 \div 2) - 1$

$C = 30 - 27$

$Y = (4 - 1) \times 2$

$A = 7 + 4$

OCTEELIA'S MESSAGE

1   10   7   5   8   4   6   3   11   7   5   2   10   9   11   0

___ ___ ___ ___ ___ ___ ___ ___ ___ ___ ___ ___ ___ ___ ___ ___

GREAT GUMSHOE! If you deciphered the hidden message, you've
got the key to an ultra-cool nest item! Simply enter the letters in
Octeelia's message backwards into the Mystery Code Machine at
Lab's Lab to get your mitts on a Bin-tastic exclusive prize.

Pssst! Want to know a secret? We've got one last special gift for you! Hold this page up to a mirror to see the secret code below. Redeem it in the Mystery Code Machine at Lab's Lab for a weevily awesome surprise!

ANSWERS

Page 14: WORDSEARCH

Page 14: WORD JUMBLES

Scrambled rooms:
Kitchen, parlour, bedroom, library, main hall, study, gallery, dining room.

Page 15: CROSSWORD

Unscrambled word: Ballroom.

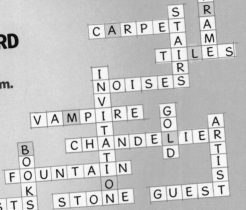

Page 21: MILLINERY MUDDLE

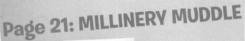

Page 26: DIRT VALLEY MAZE

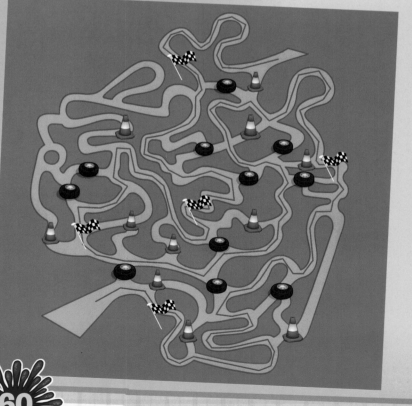

Page 28: CONE CONFUSION

A Posh **B** Tink **C** Bunty **D** Clott

Page 30: WHICH WRANGLER?

B and E

Page 30: TEST TUBE TIZZY

Kem had 2 empty test tubes left.

Page 31: SLIPPERY SUMS

$(6 \times 6) + 13 = 49$

$(16 - 8) \times 3 = 24$

$15 - (2 \times 5) = 5$

$(10 - 8) \times 3 = 6$

Page 31: PUZZLING PORTRAIT

Pages 36-37: TREASURE HUNTERS

Wink collected 4 Mulch coins and 2 jewels. Gem picked up 2 Mulch coins, 3 jewels and the treasure chest.

Pages 42-43: ROCK 'N' ROLL CODE RED

Page 48: RACING RIDDLE

Stunt (wins) – 60 secs, Trigg – 67 secs, Bing – 67 secs, Dip – 70 secs, Fab – 74 secs.

Page 49: PHOTO FINISH

Page 54: SLIME TIME!

Slam – pink, A; Pink – orange, B; Glum – purple, C; Gong – blue, E; Big Weevil – green, D.

Page 55: SUMMER SEASON

```
      B R E E Z Y
      R
      E
      L
  B E A C H        S
      L       P A L M
      F R I E N D S
      R       S U
  S P L A S H    N
  O L I     O
P O O L     T
  I
W A R M
  E
```